THE CONTESSA'S LEGACY

THE CONTESSA'S LEGACY

A NOVELLA

NORA D'ECCLESIS

RENAISSANCE PRESENTATIONS, LLC

ALSO BY NORA D'ECCLESIS

Mastering Tranquility
Tranquil Seas
Reiki Roundtable
The Retro Budget Prescription
I'm So Busy: Efficient Time Management
Lock Your Door
Adult Coloring
Equanimity and Gratitude
Tick–Borne
Spiritual Portals
Multicultural Mindfulness
Zen Rohatsu

— : —

DEDICATION

Dedicating this book to my husband, Dr. David,
is a joy and honor. His loving and compassionate
nature always provides me with incredible support
and encouragement in my work.

"Ancestor Veneration is not a matter of belief, but a matter of practice — the "practice of looking deeply into ourselves in order to recognize the presence of our ancestors..."

~ Thich Nhat Hanh

CONTENTS

CHAPTER 1

— · —

THE PUMICE RAIN - POMPEII, NAPLES 79AD

The pyroclastic flow of pumice rain stones, and lava claimed the lives of both young and old, rich, and poor. The skeletons in the five Oscan villages of ancient Pompeii were likely baked by fire from Mount Vesuvius rather than burned. A mother grabbed her child in bronchial spasm from the gases, her skin melting into the tiny frame of her beloved daughter. Her husband and son were already dead, even though hours earlier, the child warned his father to no avail.

"Papa, the fish are sick and floating on the water, and I have a pain in my chest."

The father embraced the child with love and false hope, assuring, "The earthquake happened, but we'll be alright. Finish your chores, my son. Today is your brother's wedding and the wagon will soon

1

arrive, pulled by the finest horse. You will love the sights and food. In a few hours, we will celebrate the marriage of Julia and Marcus!"

Papa shouted at Dacius to get ready because the wedding carriage was about to arrive.

"Get the horses, Dacius."

The wedding party made their way to his house, where Marcus, his son, awaited his future wife. Papa reminisced about the years when Giovanina, his brother's wife, found solace in their home after his brother's noble fight for the honor of Rome. After suffering from inflammatory joint pain and disfigurements, Papa's wife found help and support from her lovely sister-in-law. Giovanina, despite her disagreement with Papa's views on slave ownership, provided compassionate assistance to the children and even crafted the wedding attire.

Papa took great care to treat everyone fairly, ensuring that each of his forty servants and slaves received the same meals as the rest of the household. The slaves came from the lower-class Roman ranks and captured Greeks from battles.

Giovanina continuously fought for the liberation of slaves and the social advancement of the common people. Born into privilege, she underwent a unique evolution not commonly seen in women of her generation. She epitomized a beautiful maternal influence. She had raised baby Dacius, who was born to her husband, a Roman officer of high rank who had fathered a child while on campaign during one of his military deployments. Upon his return, he brought with him an infant whose mother, a slave woman, had died during delivery. Giovanina then raised baby Dacius. The laws said that Dacius, born to a slave mother, would always remain a slave himself, but Giovanina treated him as her own son. Along with Marcus, he was educated by Leander, another slave, and never treated as someone born to servitude.

Leander, the young Greek slave captured in battle, was an educated young man and now the household tutor. Dacius and Leander were part of the household and ate meals with the entire family. With joyful smiles, they celebrated their upcoming nuptial jobs. It was a peaceful home where they were treated well. However, Roman slaves in Pompeii and throughout the empire were generally not treated with compassion. The vast majority lived in sub-human shelters with little food and horrible diseases, crippled by the overuse of their joints, that even the Roman hot baths could not remedy.

Fortunately, weddings in Ancient Pompeii were

joyous affairs, commonly between young teenage couples, occasionally as young as twelve and fourteen. The couple always belonged to the same socioeconomic class. This family came from wealthy landowners growing acres of grapes and olives and selling them in urban shops in 79AD. Shops offered everything people needed or wanted: food, drink, clothing, books, and more. There were partitions between the cubbies the shopkeepers leased from the wealthy Patricians. The city was highly entrepreneurial and sophisticated.

Young bride Julia had flirted with Marcus since childhood. Playing together at shared family events brought them joy, and she was happy about marrying her love. While walking in the fields, Julia continued her thoughts, but this time out loud. "Marcus, you are my only love. We are one for eternity."

The young couple met a few days before the nuptials to follow their traditions.

"Today, it is time to sacrifice childhood toys on the altar, and as your wife, I look forward to life with you and our children."

Marcus smiled and danced in the fields with his future bride, a woman who made his heart pound. He was grateful the parents had agreed to the nuptials. He then sacrificed his childish belongings even though it was not the custom, as men were the superior and dominant forces in their homes in 79AD.

"Julia, join me in gathering flowers for the crown you'll wear at our ceremony." "Yes, my love, over there. The cooler days at the end of summer bring the bloom of my favorite flowers. That lemon myrtle tree has the most exquisite flower."

The Roman marriage planned for tomorrow, which never arrived, was meant to be spiritual and legal through Confarreatio. The witnesses would consist of family, friends, and an official. The couple would ride in a wagon, leading a procession through the ancient streets of Pompeii to the celebration hall. They envisioned themselves dressed in white tunics, with the bride's head adorned with flowers and a red veil, waving to onlookers while riding the wagon. Riding on a marriage wagon decorated with erotic art like frescoes of the time, they envisioned a joyful future surrounded by their beloved family and relatives.

Julia was fourteen, and Marcus was seventeen. Pompeii, a comfortable resort city, welcomed tourists with a variety of food and drinks, appealing to people from all backgrounds. It was the most esteemed of all resort towns, attracting the most affluent individuals of its era.

Patricians and plebeians converged at the Bay of Naples to swim in the sea and celebrate in the villas, engaging in excessive activities like visiting brothels and drinking all day and night.

Unfortunately, it was already too late. No Richter scale or media warned the many who perished in the Fall of 79AD. It took Pliney the Younger, a writer and witness, an additional twenty-five years to finally document the horror he witnessed in Naples, including the death of his Uncle Pliney, who had saved countless lives as an admiral. It was a visual trauma, complete with physical distress unknown to any human until that day.

The joy turned to fear as the Salacia family looked up in horror as the pumice rock rained down on them from Mt. Vesuvius. Papa quickly revised his instructions. "Leander, prepare the cart with my son and his bride and take Marcus and my other young children to the ocean."

"Marcus, these are the coins chosen for your wedding. Leave immediately and board a ship heading to Naples. I will find your mother and join you. She is at the bakery getting your wedding cake."

"Go! Take your little brother and your little sister with you. Children, obey Marcus as you would me."

The young couple and their siblings followed instructions and got on the wagon while the slaves guided the horses by running alongside. Over fifty household members were part of the group. The young children watched in horror as the horse reared and fled back into the city. Crying and screaming, the children raced towards the city, desperately searching for their parents, never to be seen again.

The family of five, destined to be the survivors, ran on foot toward the safety of the sea.

"Cover your mouth, Julia. Please help her, Giovanina."

"Leander, run faster to the ships and secure our passage. Take a bag of wedding coins engraved with the Imperial Emperor. I can see the Royal Naval fleet. Run faster than the horse, my friend."

"Tell the Navy we are the familia Salacia. Take my tunic and wear it as a free man so they will give you respect and passage."

The other forty or so slaves and plebeians from the Salacia Villa also fled the city, escaping the hellish fumes.

The family of five embarked on the ship in the Bay of Naples, sailing fifteen miles to safety. Once everyone was safely on the ship, it was decided that the marriage would occur immediately. Giovanina, who was only a decade older than the family she had cared for and adored, kissed each family member.

She announced, "Marcus and Julia are now officially married, witnessed by our familia."

Marcus, overcome with grief and loss, kissed his wife while tears flowed down his face. In response, Julia's voice, choked with emotion, said, "My love, your green eyes are just as beautiful as you. It's time for us to look into them as we move on, never looking back at the destruction."

Marcus's response was filled with the intensity of true love and soulmates as he held tight. Holding his bride close, Marcus announced, "With our family as witnesses, we are officially married. Only fifteen more miles remain until we reach Neapolitan soil, where our new life as a family begins."

Once on land again, Marcus took command. "Take the other bags of coins, Leander. I trust you as a brother. Secure lodging for all of us." Leander bought numerous fertile acres of farmland, including a spacious villa, where the survivors, luckier than others, thrived and prospered.

The men and women who had been in the Pompeii Salacia Villa reunited with the family and joined the household. They were all free men now, with much to look forward to. Thousands of survivors arrived in Naples, where they were welcomed as emigrants from the volcanic destruction of Pompeii. The Salacia family discovered that the government planned to use recovered coins and artwork to aid in the reconstruction efforts for the survivors of the Pompeii tragedy in Naples. The Roman government funded the emigration and helped all establish new lives.

The Villa Salacia was renowned for never having enslaved individuals, and subsequent generations upheld this tradition. Giovanina's early influence fostered a harmonious and egalitarian atmosphere in the household. The Imperial Emperor relocated the assets from those who perished in Pompeii to Naples to assist the thousands of emigrants. Their ancestors still carry on the generational legacy of those families.

Pliny the Elder, the fleet's admiral, was not the captain of the ship on which the five survivors were sailing. Nevertheless, he is credited for saving countless lives as the Commander of the Navy. Pliny sailed to Stabiae on one of his ships to rescue others. Tragically, he met a horrific death while trying to save them, succumbing to fumes that devastated his frail heart and lungs. Pliny the Elder published many books that served as a comprehensive encyclopedia for its time and earned him admiration for his brilliance. Pliny was admired as both a hero and a patriot.

The surviving five, which included Marcus, Julia Salacia, Giovanina, and her adopted son Dacius, embraced each other as a loving family. When they set sail, Dacius sought permission to become one of the 232 oarsmen on the Royal Navy ship. Giovanina appeared to comprehend Dacius' desire to enlist in the military and, more significantly, to be surrounded by like-minded individuals. Giovanina managed the new household, while Leander and Marcus oversaw their olive empire as land barons.

Marcus and his wife, Julia, had multiple children. Together with the rest of the household's children, they discovered the importance of staying in the present moment, leading to a life filled with joy and gratitude.

Following Pompeii, Roman history was marked by frequent and brutal wars. Numerous nations merged their cultures and took over Naples, and eventually, peace was established. It's possible that the future descendants of Pompeii's residents will pursue a better life over the next thousand years.

It is difficult to determine the number of generations that followed the Salacia Family, but during the 15th century, a more refined Naples arose, continuing the story.

Following the Renaissance, explorers initiated the search for new lands and trade routes, resulting in the explorer's food exchange for exotic fruits and vegetables. In the early 1500s, tomatoes were brought back from the New World to Western Europe, and it was in Spain and Italy where they first arrived. However, it was the French who initially incorporated tomatoes into sauces.

The fertile volcanic soil from Mt. Vesuvius gave rise to the San Marzano tomato, which thrives above the Bay of Naples. This plum-type tomato is sweet with few seeds and little acidic content. Vesuvius, now mostly calm, oversees the tomato vineyards that yield the ideal sauce for the beloved Margherita pizza in Naples.

Italian cuisine always centered around family, food, and old-fashioned fun, including the occasional pizza party. People worldwide began enjoying pizza together, making it a group activity. The pizza is freshly made by a skilled pizzaiolo, with the ingredients arranged in a traditional artistic manner. The initial pizza in Pompeii was likely a simple white pizza with only oil and cheese on the crust, but the introduction of tomatoes from the new world transformed it into the beloved dish it is today. Naples, Italy, is the birthplace of the Margherita pizza.

The Italian unification consolidated the city-states into the Kingdom of Italy, also known as the Risorgimento, which King Umberto I championed. He was married to Queen Margherita of Savoy, a popular Queen Consort, who recommended a city tour as part of the 1889 unification campaign. Before the King and Queen's trip to Naples, the Queen asked for traditional Italian food and requested pizza from the Chef. Chef Raffaele Esposito is said to have organized a commemorative feast for the unification, where he crafted a magnificent pizza adorned with the hues of Unified Italy – red tomatoes, white mozzarella, and green basil. To this day, Margherita Pizza remains the name used for this style and toppings in any country where it is marketed.

Many towns, villages, mountain peaks, and art museums were named after the Queen, but not as much for her husband Umberto, who was assassinated in 1900, causing unrest. The Royal Blue Bloods lacked popularity in Western Europe as new politics emerged.

Despite that, King Umberto celebrated his Silver

Wedding Anniversary with Margherita. In 1893, a villa was excavated in ancient Pompeii ruins, and the excavators named it 'The House of the Silver Wedding' in honor of the wedding anniversary of the King and Queen. Although they likely didn't visit the Pompeii house after it was excavated, they were informed about its Corinthian columns, gardens, and pools. The King and Queen Margherita successfully had a son and descendants who continued to rule until the formation of the Italian Republic in 1946.

Chapter 2

— · —

The Contessa Exits Naples

Grandmother Angelina grew up in a luxurious castle near Naples, complete with the materialistic opulence of its era. Marrying early was a way to ensure her social standing and well-being, given the precarious circumstances of the Italian royal elite. The marriage to the Count granted her the title of Contessa, which she refused to relinquish even in death. The older husband also ensured the line of succession by having three babies within their first ten years of marriage. In a single night, the Count passed away, collapsing before he even touched the ground. It could have been a major heart attack or the staff preparing a meal fit for a king, and we know how many felt about kings.

To stay safe during the uncertain times of the early 1900s, the Contessa and her children were instructed to immigrate to America and promptly placed on a ship. Leaving her home and friends without warning was never a topic of conversation. As the King of Italy had just been assassinated, the Americans allowed her to immigrate and welcomed many members of Italian households.

The journey to America was brutal, even for those in first class, and having young children made it even worse. The Contessa was stoic and persevered as she waved and cried at the sight of the Statue of Liberty in New York Harbor.

Relatives already settled in the USA warmly received Contessa Angelina. They soon introduced her to her next husband, a man who, like herself, had immigrated and was of Italian and perhaps some French descent. After marriage, they traveled to his homestead in middle America, and that emigration proved joyful. They made a simple life together, and the marriage produced three more children. Contessa's birth privilege was kept a secret from Grand-PaPa for a long time, but he had always been aware. Whenever there was a death or wedding, the recent immigrants from the old country would walk past him and kneel before his wife, kissing her hand and ring. The Contessa would forever be Angelina, his wife and mother to their children.

Living in America, she had three sons with the Count, who was a decade older than their American siblings. Under the same roof, they all shared a dreadful sibling rivalry. Her first husband's sons regained Italian citizenship and visited their mother only on rare occasions. On a particular journey, the Contessa questioned her eldest son, Stephano, about his decision to leave his siblings and return to their homeland from America.

"Mama, in Italy, we are treated with the respect owed to our father because he was a good man and was loved in his village. The people are compassionate, much less competitive, and less greedy. My fistfights with my younger brothers were horrible. We never felt comfortable with your new family. The myth of Romulus killing his brother Remus because they disagreed on which hill to build their new city of ancient Rome played over in my head. So, after writing to the relatives who remained in Naples, and after my twenty-third birthday, we returned to a lovely country with great opportunities. At the time, you were busy with your new family. We have a good life, loving wives and children, and the traditions and rituals of an ancient culture. Perhaps the thought that moving away from our stress will eliminate it is inaccurate, and decisions made in haste aren't always the best path. But in the end, it worked out okay. We write and visit our siblings and enjoy the Italian country of our birth, with its majestic mountains and oceans."

Now living on the opposite coast from where he was born in Naples, Stephano enjoyed a lovely life in Bari, Puglia. The sons of the former Count and Contessa ran a magnificent restaurant near the Basilica of Saint Nicholas, where they also sold street foods. The kids helped to make the orecchiette pasta by hand, showing their potential as future restauranteurs. Children filled the streets, playing while old men engaged in animated political discussions. The ocean and beach were so clean and enjoyed by residents and tourists. Why would anyone want to leave? The answer is always the same. The choices made, preferences considered, and the individual quest for the best quality of life.

In America, every Sunday during family visits, Grandmother Angelina, The Contessa, would sit on a dark red velvet sofa with all the grandkids surrounding her. It was a command performance and tradition after they enjoyed the medium-rare lamb roast with mint jelly and the traditional ravioli handmade the night before. The pizza squares and salad started the meal. The day concluded with the cousins playing in her backyard, complete with swings and a sandbox for the younger ones.

Today Grandma seemed nostalgic as she began with a story about the Spanish flu and the importance of using bleach while cleaning. The elders and parents gathered in the great room as she discussed the 1918 Pandemic, known as the Spanish flu but likely not originating in Spain. The 1918 pandemic did kill millions, but Grandma was sure it would never happen again. However, in case masks were needed again, she stored bleach and muslin cloth in the basement.

Later, the men stepped away for some homemade whisky and stogie cigars. The wives indulged in serene cups of espresso and tiramisu, and Grandma reveled in the company of her grandchildren. Political beliefs varied among the adults, resulting in animated discussions. The day concluded with hugs and double kisses, even among the men. The Contessa's family dealt with generational conflicts in their own unique way, but they consistently demonstrated the love taught in her home.

Michael was always the one to ask questions first. He was curious and the most vocal of the grandchildren. "Grandma, what was that pizza called?"

"It is called Margherita Pizza. I thought it would

be a great idea to make Margherita Pizza from Naples, Italy, again and enjoy it more frequently during our Sunday dinners." The Contessa kept on recounting her tale...

"While walking near the city one night, the cool air smelled like home. I stumbled upon an American pizza storefront less than fifty feet away because of the tempting aroma. It smelled just like what my mother made from scratch, the Neapolitan pizza. The order was somehow accepted despite my using broken Italian. Margherita pizza and drinks, but hold the forks! The counter person weighed the generous square piece of pizza on the large paper plate. The weight of the pie was given in grams since it was sold by weight."

"Next, they included the drink and calculated the total price. Biting the crisp crust was so reminiscent of mother's pie. However, the mozzarella tasted milkier and stretched around our mouths, swirling around the delectable sauce with tomato chunks perfectly seasoned with fresh basil. The crust was airy like clouds. Blowing to cool the sizzling hot square was necessary before taking the initial heavenly bite. The delicious taste reminded me of ancient ancestors relaxing on lavish furniture, enjoying meals in their Pompeiian courtyards."

What a fabulous way to break bread with friends and family! At that moment, they decided to make it a part of our traditional meals together as a family here in America. The grandchildren were now salivating again.

By avoiding the politics of the early 1900s, the Contessa forfeited her title as an Italian blue-blood royalty. Despite being young, she married and had more children. Grandpa, a man from a nearby village or another province near Naples, was truly remarkable. But his Italian became incomprehensible after a stroke, just ten years into his marriage. The stroke left him and the whole family devastated by his paralysis. They all contributed to his care with the love of a large family taught to value the elders.

As more and more immigrants came from Italy, Grandma and her sons welcomed them, secured employment, and threw parties for the newcomers who had just arrived. Angelina wanted them to know her family and be friends before adapting to the new culture and language. Dozens of chickens would be barbecued, accompanied by the consumption of homemade wine called Barberone and the feasting on generous servings of lasagna. The presence of a pizza slice served as a joyous reminder that their traditions could travel with them. It was the best of times knowing they had a community of loving neighbors who became chosen family.

Lydia was fidgeting because she knew her questions for the day and wanted to ask them. As the oldest female grandchild, she might have inherited the title of Contessa, but that was not in the cards, as even Italy no longer honored the royal family. "Grandma, tell us more about the history of Naples and ancient Pompeii. Did anyone survive the Vesuvius eruption and lava?"

"Yes, Lydia. According to the elders, people survived the eruption by going to the sea or leaving the city for safer places. We learn from experience that our lives are more important than our possessions." The Contessa had an agenda and went directly to it. "Tell us how you are doing in school in this wonderful country. It is important to be a good citizen. Your education in America is the start of a great opportunity."

Lydia listened to her cousins drone on about their good grades and achievements, but the picture-perfect life the Contessa described did not seem to fit Lydia's experience.

"Grandma!"

"Wait your turn, Lydia; I want to discuss our Christmas Eve dinner meal and the preparations."

Realizing Grandma's insistence on setting up the family Christmas preparations first, Lydia and Michael gathered the family to get supplies for taking notes.

A tin box held the recipes on stained index cards. Lydia sat, pencil in hand and large index cards ready, preparing to write the Contessa's legacies again. This one would be titled The Feast of the Seven Fishes, even though it wasn't officially a feast day in their faith.

"Call Grandma, Michael, and tell her we are ready." Michael smiled and responded by calling both the Contessa and his father, Sergio.

The Contessa Angelina was a regal woman, always sitting and standing with good posture and impeccably dressed. Like her mother, she was tall and thin for her age. Her hair was pulled back in a bun and held with a 10k gold hairpin from Italy. Her green eyes were a defining physical characteristic, and today, they seemed more emerald than hazel. Grandma began her Christmas Eve tale by recalling how things were done in her childhood.

"Planning is very important, children. It started a few weeks before Christmas. The Italian markets sold large, thick pieces of salted codfish. We purchased the superior extra line-caught cod, and, of course, it was covered in salt, so it required a rinse each day, in fact, several times a day. After placing it in a large pot of water three times a day, we doubled the usual rinse. Then, on the morning of Christmas Eve, it was rinsed one last time by the strongest members of the family because the pots were so heavy, and then placed in a simmering pot of water to cook. When it was tender, the pieces were filtered on cheesecloth. The tender white flakes of cod were placed on serving platters with an inch of olive oil, olives, and red roasting peppers. Only then was it called Baccala! Then, the family members went to different areas to prepare the other fish, so we had seven types."

"Michael, ask your father to translate, as I want to speak in my native dialect."

"Yes, Grandma". Sergio took Lydia's pad and began to write from memory.

"The first step in preparing the squid involved removing the ink from the mantle and extracting the beak. The rings are cut and then simmered gently in marinara sauce."

Sergio couldn't control himself. "The smelts required ventilation, kids. Boy, did they stink." Grandma did not find the laughter amusing, so she handed the pad back to Michael this time.

"OK, back to the smelts. These beautiful, tiny fish, similar to salmon, lived in fresh water and the sea at some point. They were not expensive, so they could feed extra unexpected quests and, once fried, were delicious."

"Lydia, do you like anchovies?"

"No way, Grandma. They are salty and have little spines."

"When the fishermen pull them in from the sea in their nets, they are exquisite green with a hint of blue. They swim off the coast of the Cinque Terra Liguria, where I first saw them. Perhaps that explains why my eyes share the same color. I love them, especially in the marinara sauce for the puttanesca."

"Eels are picked up fresh on Christmas Eve and sold alive, so only one member of the family prepares them. It is worse than plucking a chicken, and they bite! Sergio put his hand in the bag one night and learned the hard way! After cleaning, they are dipped in egg and flour and fried until the meat is white and delicious."

"Shrimp are the most expensive and are always eaten raw in a cocktail sauce. Clams and mussels are quickly cooked until tender and then coated in a lemon butter sauce. It takes more time to clean them and remove sand than cooking time."

"Hey, wait a minute. That's more than seven." Grandma motioned for her son Sergio to be silent.

"Your father always said the anchovies don't count." Perhaps she even smiled after what she believed to be a humorous remark.

"Lydia, please read it back."

"How does this sound, Grandma?"

The Contessa's response was classic Italian. She placed her hands together as if in prayer and rocked back and forth in approval.

Finally, it was Lydia's turn to comment. The agony of listening to the others talk about their joys and being bored with taking notes on the Feast of the Seven Fishes only exasperated her pain. "After Dad died, Mother had to move to the other side of town. This meant a new school and making new friends if you could call them that. The rest of our cousins remained in this area and had access to things not accessible to us."

Grandma rose, holding her hand up to stop the conversation, and said with animation, "Stop this talk. We can continue after the children go out to play."

Michael and Lydia remained. They were close cousins who shared common interests and opinions. "Lydia is correct," Michael stated as he spoke first. "Neighborhoods define the lines and the belief that guidance is unnecessary, unwanted, or undeserved by blue-collar ethnic communities."

Lydia frowned at the term blue collar. "My dad was blue collar and worked long hours doing wonderful work, but was never invited to play tennis or golf with his customers. Immigrants are often told to know their place and ensure their children follow suit."

Despite her stern expression, the Contessa appeared to have tears in her eyes. Michael and Lydia stood up to search for their friends, Owen and Joe. Despite her expectations, she realized their legacy was far from the idyllic vision she had in mind.

Seated by the lake, the friends chewed on cattails as if they were smoking while Michael shared his plan to join the Navy and travel, finding purpose through service. Joe described the joy and honor of serving God as an altar server. Owen wanted the bullies to leave him alone and stop calling him rotund. Despite this, he succeeded as a certified accountant, resulting in a joyful marriage and a prosperous profession.

Lydia jumped over the rocks, wetting her shoes and socks. She was sure of a lovely future and was determined to work hard and make it happen someday, with or without help. Laughing together, they found solace from their worries and cherished their friendship, at least for that day. The Contessa's promised life appeared full of possibilities.

CHAPTER 3

BULLY AND BEAST OF ENMITY

He walked out of the room, his heart filled with grief. His lasting memory of it will be as the dying room. The attendants, attempting to maintain a serious facade yet clearly exhausted and uninterested at 5 am, positioned themselves next to the gurney, prepared to transfer a corpse to the morgue. In the silent darkness, a cold metal slab and locker awaited the decision of a grieving family from the West Coast – to incinerate her or take her body home for burial.

Joe's childhood friend, Owen, stood by his side, offering support in their shared grief. A light had gone out, a connection to their childhood.

They had gone to what some claimed was a party, the reunion of their high school class. While others enjoyed the party, the three braced themselves for long-delayed confrontations. During the reunion party, Lydia broke away and spoke a few words to a classmate. Her loud voice and aggressive hand gestures made it seem like she was about to hit him. The security guards forcefully brought her down to the ballroom floor, appearing excessive as they disabled her ability to escape by targeting her knees from behind.

Turning away from the conversation and her Waldorf salad, the friends assumed she was drunk as she silently walked towards the classmate, ignoring Owen and Joe. With a clenched fist, she struck his jaw so hard that blood dripped down onto his shoe. His face showed shock as he glanced at the blood on his expensive European suit. Rico, the victim, shot a piercing look at Lydia just before the security team intervened and grabbed her. "You bitch!" "Stay on the wrong side of the tracks, where the soot goes!" The tone and words from his youth had slipped out as the bully within still existed.

Lydia was quickly pulled up, restrained, and transported by the local police station to a basement holding cell. She was booked, processed, and held for arraignment.

Owen stood in the doorway, giving advice to the doctors coming and going regarding her allergies. Then, the color drained from Owen's checks as he realized the obvious.

"Lydia is dead."

Joe nodded sagely.

"Yes, she's dead." He hesitated, seemingly grappling with internal conflict, before uttering five life-altering words. "Why did Lydia comment suicide?"

Joe, a childhood classmate and now priest, made the sign of the cross as Lydia's body was carried head first past the friends in the hall. Father Giuseppe, also known as Father Joe, turned to Owen and said with a cracked voice, "We need to contact Lydia's son, Thomas, and daughter-in-law, Cathleen." Owen reluctantly agreed, although he grimaced at the thought. Father Joe sat in the car, watching the hearse leave the police station driveway as he prepared to inform Lydia's son. However, Owen and Joe suddenly agreed that they should postpone calling Lydia's son for a few hours, as they knew from previous late-night calls that they were never good news.

They planned to inform Lydia's son and dear cousin, Mike, in the morning since they were the only family to contact. Mike served as a Navy officer deployed on an aircraft carrier. The surprise of her sudden death would leave him devastated and overwhelmed with grief.

In the morning, Father Joe made the call that is always gut-wrenching when someone dies in their prime.

"Thomas, this is Father Joe, and Owen is here with me. We have some difficult words that come with a heavy heart. Your mother has passed away. Her death came early this morning, and we were with her from the moment the doctors feared her life signs were fading."

"Oh my God, Father, what happened? Was it an auto accident in that rental sports car? How did she die?" Thomas' sorrow became audible as he spoke the word, Mama, which Joe could hear.

The questions and even fewer answers could wait.

"This is all I know. The young officer in charge went to the diner and ordered a turkey burger, fries, and a salad. Your mother happily ate it. She was aware of a potential food allergy, so authorities are considering the incident at the reunion dinner as a suicide. Her allergy emerged during the middle of the night, well after the meal. According to the local police, her body was covered in hives the size of cell phones, which they described as horrific.

"Lydia urgently requested help because she felt

itchy and nauseous, so someone summoned an ambulance. Fluid filled her lungs, causing her blood pressure to drop. The capillaries leaked, allowing blood serum to fill the lungs and impede her breathing. She passed away within a few minutes."

Anaphylaxis is a gruesome condition that few comprehend. Staring at the Heavens, Lydia's green eyes remained wide open in death.

At Thomas' request, Father Joe began organizing the memorial funeral service. According to the post-mortem, Lydia's death was self-inflicted and not caused by intoxication. Her loved ones were aware of her walnut allergy. At the reunion, Lydia knowingly ate a salad that supposedly had nuts, and it's uncertain whether she called for help when her allergy symptoms emerged in the jail cell. When the guards discovered her, she was on the verge of anaphylactic shock.

"Why Owen? Why now, after all these years, did she retaliate against the classmate who was accused of such horrific bullying way back in high school?"

That question may never be answered, but she did it cold stone sober, and now her faith-based religion will not allow a burial funeral service. Father Joe had a plan in mind as he began with the cremation and then took care of the legal formalities to bring her ashes back home to the West.

Owen pondered how best to memorialize her, and Joe responded with a Zen ceremony in the monastery where she meditated.

"Thomas, it seems her last word was baby. What are your thoughts on that?"

"That doesn't make sense now, but maybe it will in the future."

Everyone, including Father Joe, wondered why she ate a salad with nuts despite her allergy and why she attended the reunion to revisit her past horrors.

"Let us pray, Thomas, and accept her passing."

Father Joe began the 23rd Psalm.

Chapter 4

Zen Funeral 49 Days

Driving up the coast on the scenic Pacific Coast Highway seemed like it should be a vacation drive than the ride to bury his mother. It left Lydia's son, Thomas, Cathleen, his wife, and little Sophia, their daughter, somewhat disturbed. Thomas shifted his thoughts to happier days, driving to visit his parents.

Thomas put the top down on his convertible and looked at his lovely wife and their amazing daughter. He knew he was blessed with a loving family and that his wife felt the same. They met in college, fell in love, and a year later, were married, with Father Joe officiating. The small church was neutral territory by their university, so there was no family drama. The usual question was posed: Why hurry into it while you're still young? Thomas and Cathleen were sure of their love, which led to more understanding inquiries and guidance, and in the end, both families happily joined together to celebrate as they had planned.

Father Joe, Owen, and Diane flew in for the ceremony, followed by an exquisite reception paid for by Cathleen's parents, as per tradition. Their parents' traditions remained significant to them.

Thomas and Cathleen, both born in the West, were so unique that kindergarten teachers would ask their classes who were born in California, and only they would raise their hands.

"Thomas, pay attention to the road. You're lost in memories of our early days in college."

Snuggling with her little stuffed animals in her car seat, Sophia commented, "Oh, mommy, that's mushy."

"OK, honey, Daddy and I will tell you about our days on boogie boards as we drive to Grandma and Grandpa's former house."

Her husband Sebastian's departure, Lydia's addictions, and a few infidelities led to the abandonment of their empty old house. A troubled upbringing can instill in a child the ability to make different choices, steering clear of the ancestral pain.

Following Buddhist traditions, the Zen Funeral occurred precisely forty-nine days after Lydia's death.

So, at forty-nine days, Father Joe and Owen arrived in Northern California to bury Lydia and celebrate their lifelong friendship.

"Owen, we need to go directly to the Monastery from the airport and make final arrangements."

"Is there a way for you to say some prayers, Joe?"

"No, we can't do that. Rules are rules."

"I think Lydia would have wanted it."

"This is the Zen Monastery where Lydia did yoga, sat in meditations, and went to a weekly spiritual liturgy. It was Lydia's choice and spiritual home. We must respect their Zen traditions."

"Joe, I understand spirituality, but not religion. Growing up in a faith-based religion, she might have wished for readings, maybe not just for herself but also for Thomas."

"Well, Owen, without a note or a Last Will and Testament from Lydia, it's important to acknowledge her dedication to meditation in this monastery and the valuable services they offer."

"Oh, here comes the family. Let me just be sure the flowers are perfect on their altar, next to the incense and lovely Buddha statue."

"Yes, thanks, Owen."

"Sophia, there's my big girl. Good morning, Thomas and Cathleen." Sophia ran to Father Joe with a big hug, silently questioning whether we'd be all right without Grandma.

Michael, a heartbroken cousin, also arrived early and embraced Thomas with the love of a blood relative. Without asking questions, he sat silently beside his wife, Joan. His years of military service in the navy had shaped him into Lydia's favorite relative, a strong, silent gentleman. Michael, who served as an XO on an aircraft carrier, was allowed to take leave for the funeral.

The fragrance of the flowers and incense preceded the entrance to the Zendo. In the Zen tradition, incense was burned to purify and sweeten the air. Multiple gong strikes signaled the start, as everyone found their seats—some on chairs, while others, members of the Sangha, chose zafus and zabutons, small and large pillows.

Owen couldn't resist a quick whisper about sitting on pillows in the Burmese position for long periods.

"How do they do that? It looks very painful."

"All I know is that my mother spent hours meditating on those pillows, Owen. It must be an acquired skill."

Assisted by a junior monk and encouraged to use the milder Burmese position, Thomas walked to the pillows and sat with his family.

Upon entering the room, the Zen master bowed to the Buddha on the altar, and everyone stood up. Roshi Chandler greeted the attendees by putting his hands in ghassho and bowing, receiving bows in return.

He then donned his Rokusu over his head and around his neck. As he approached the altar, the monks could be heard explaining aspects of the service to guests:

"The meditation practice starts with the ancient gong's sound and the scent of incense filling the zendo. We walk mindfully, one hand closed, the other protecting it with shashu, fully aware of each step and the precision of our motion, and engage in the ancient practice of circumambulation, just like the Buddha did. Starting with the ball of the big toe hitting the ground, we merge walking meditation with zazen, bringing the tranquility of sitting meditation into motion."

"We stay in the present, not thinking of anything. We are mindful. Each step is breathing in and breathing out in synergy with our kinhin."

"We rise from zazen, seated meditation, by tilting the torso forward upright about ninety degrees, then extending the hips and knees. We stand on a mid-foot landing, letting go of everything and controlling our breath as we move forward in peace and equanimity. Kinhin, our walking meditation, is practiced with our eyes at half-mast, looking not at the walls of the zendo or the birds in the trees through the window."

"When we hear a sound, we simply hear it. So, the chirping bird does not excite us and break the walking meditation, nor does the fire truck racing down the street with sirens blaring. We do not look up or take note to tell the other meditators how lovely the sound of the bird. We allow the concept of bird chirping, then proceed in kinhin. While walking indoors, we might be tempted to cut corners, but this is not the best way, as zens do not cut corners in walking meditation or life."

"Walking now, one foot extending in front of the other, mindfully walking as we meditate with others in a community of spirituality. Today we will exit the solitude of the meditation hall as we walk single file out the door and move toward an outdoor walking meditation. The family of the deceased will follow the Monks."

"Picture a gigantic labyrinth, much like the one found in Notre Dame de Chartres in Paris. Our labyrinth sits in an area of lush trees and gardens. It might be said that walking into a labyrinth is a metaphor for walking toward your core. It is a spiritual experience."

"Our labyrinth is unicursal. The way out is the same as the way in. It is not a maze or puzzle to be solved. It is a labyrinth is a path in and out. As we walk in silent meditation into the labyrinth, we pause at the entrance to center ourselves. We might be so intent on getting to the end that we miss the subtle sounds, sights, and smells of nature. If we are mindful, we notice the small signs that others have passed this way before us, such as a footprint, a memento left lovingly behind, or a stone dislodged by a wayward boot. We notice our inclination to make everything perfect again, pick up the stone, and erase the footprint."

"We acknowledge the sacredness of the space, cleansed by many feet, silently stepping and spiraling through the small path. We feel connected to all who have traveled this path, especially to those on it together in community meditation, our sangha. We then return to the meditation center with the intention set toward our more spiritual core and the silence of seated meditation. Satori, or the experience of awakening, is a little closer."

Little Sophia kept pace with the rest of the Sangha and seemed awed by their walking meditation tradition. Her eyes looked down as instructed, but tears fell on both cheeks. The cremation urn that carried her beloved grandmother would remain here near the labyrinth in a Buddhist mausoleum.

"Daddy, did grandma have a Rokusu?"

"Yes, honey, and she left it to you."

"I loved her so much, Daddy." The child's comments brought tears to everyone's eyes.

After taking the Buddhist Precepts, Lydia devoted an entire year to hand-sewing her own Rokusu, a small cloth symbolizing the rag Siddhartha used while meditating under the bodhi tree before enlightenment.

The Rokusu, worn by the Zen monk and master, is a replica of a garment worn by the Buddha as he sat to achieve enlightenment. Its original intention was to warm the Buddha while he gazed at a rectangular patchwork of rice fields. It is traditionally a sewn patchwork, black in front and white in back, made by those about to take Zen precepts or be ordained. The Bodhi Tree, also known as the tree of awakening, is located in Bodh Gaya and is believed to be the sacred fig tree where the Buddha achieved enlightenment.

The Roshi then went to the altar and bowed to the Buddha, explaining that he was bowing to the Buddha in himself, not a statue.

The Roshi placed additional incense on the altar in a circular motion and then again turned to his Sangha chanting:

Namo Tassa

Bhagavato Arahato

Samma Sambuddhassa

He explained the Mahayana tradition and Buddhist teachings of impermanence. The monks will now chant the Heart Sutra, paying homage to Avalokiteshvara, the Bodhisattva of compassion. Her heart contains no guile, judgment, resentment, anger, or disdain, just compassion. During the chaos of life, when storms are raging and lives seem cold and bare, Avalokiteshvara is the Buddhist Saint.

From The Middle Length Discourses of the Buddha:

One is not a brahmin by birth,

Nor by birth a non-brahmin.

By action is one a brahmin,

By action is one a non-brahmin

A Bodhisattva finds joy in bodhicitta, the enlightened mind. Compassionate and empathic, they extend compassion to help all sentient beings. Roshi remarked that Lydia repeated, "One is not a Brahmin by birth" each time she sat to meditate.

"We will delve into their teachings today as a tribute to Lydia's love for Dharma chats."

"Manjushri is the Bodhisattva of transcendent wisdom. He is usually shown as a male with a flaming sword in his right hand, cutting ignorance. He sits on a lion rather than fighting it. He is depicted as a noble giant with a sword that cuts down ignorance through ego and duality. As a genius himself, Manjushri helps with learning skills and memory. In his other hand, he holds the Diamond and Heart Sutras on a lotus stem, keeping the books of perfection and wisdom close to him."

"Jizo is the guardian of children and women in childbirth and travel, offering a peaceful passage. Jizo Bosatsu watches over both children and travelers. The Jizo replicas are made of stone for longevity and are found on trails with more stones piled near them."

"Lydia placed Jizo statues in her car and home on walking paths before Sophia's birth."

Hearing these words during the service, Sophia held tighter to her mother's hand.

"Jizo statues assist with childbirth and promote fertility for parents. Jizo replicas wear red hats and bibs in Japan to protect against illness and evil. To support the little Jizo stone statues, people place small stones and stonewalls near or above them."

"Lydia built her stones as high as they would stand in honor of her son Thomas, Cathleen, and especially Sophia. Walk the paths of her homestead tonight and view her beliefs with an open heart."

Avalokitesvara is the Mahayana Zen Buddhist bodhisattva of compassion. The Jesuit missionaries nicknamed this saint the mercy goddess. The Lotus Sutra teaches us that chanting their name will free all from suffering. The Zen monks taught these ideas to the Catholic missionaries.

Kan Ji Zai Bo Sa Gyo Jin Han Nya Ha Mi Ta

The Roshi said, "Finally, two of Lydia's favorite Dharma teachings include *The Mustard Seed* and *The Parable of the Poison Arrow*."

"The Mustard Seed teaches us how a young woman, a mother, carried a lifeless child to the Buddha and requested that the Buddha bring the child back to life. With compassion, the Buddha directed the woman to retrieve the mustard seed from a dwelling in the village that had not experienced death. She carried out the task, soon comprehended the teachings, and despite her grief, she became a member of the Sangha."

The Parable of the Poison Arrow teaches the lesson of the futility of asking questions and more questions. A poison arrow shoots a person, but before they allow friends to remove the arrow, they ask questions

Who shot the arrow?

Why did they shoot me with an arrow?

Which direction did it come from?

In Zen, it is believed that the person who is shot will probably die before receiving answers to their questions.

Roshi took a deep breath and explained how vital these teachings were to the funeral service.

"We will never know why Lydia left us, and more questions will not bring us peace. Death and grief are with all who are sentient beings."

"Mommy, I love this. It is as beautiful as our service."

"Yes, Sophia, we'll be back to explore Grandma's spiritual tradition and learn more about what she believed and discovered."

Mindful of the granddaughter's respectful questions, Reverend Chandler asked her to sit near him on a zafu. Roshi took her little hands and said, "Your grandmother believed in helping those who needed her and was a very compassionate woman. She knew the importance of loving her family and friends and advocated for justice." While continuing to hold her hand, Roshi spoke more of Lydia's quest to stay in the present and leave traumas in the past.

Roshi, Chandler, and Sophia then stood asking all to join them as they recited what he had taught Lydia and all his Sangha's for so many years.

May I become, at all times, both now and forever, a protector for those who lack protection, a guide for those who have lost their way, a ship for those without light, a place of refuge for those who lack shelter, and a servant to all in need.

Zen Master Roshi invited Father Joe to say a few words he dedicated to Christian Scripture. A Tibetan guest who also knew Lydia explained the *Tibetan Book of the Dead* and the significance of the forty-nine days. Roshi concluded the service by asking for a respectful period of grief to begin after the forty-nine days.

As Roshi concluded the service by removing his Rokusu, everyone present regretted not knowing Lydia more intimately—her joys, sorrows, and the reasons behind her choices. With her innocent and compassionate nature, Sophia likely understood her better than anyone. Like previous generations of grandchildren, she, too, gained wisdom from her ancestors. The twinkle in Sophia's eyes at Buddha's altar made it clear to her parents that she would pursue meditation.

CHAPTER 5

— · —

ATTEND REUNION MAYBE

Lydia had been mentally rehearsing alibis for the school reunion at her home in Northern California. Spring arrived, signaling a fresh start, and she found herself torn about going to the high school reunion. There's plenty to hate about school and more to hate about the idea of a school reunion if the school experience was terrible. Adult maturity fails to overcome the cliques and social strata of schoolyard peer interaction, as reconnecting with old acquaintances only provides evidence to support this theory, especially for those with a negative experience.

Moreover, arranging a reunion for individuals only connected by geography seemed silly. If she had been concerned about losing contact with specific individuals, she likely wouldn't have become distant from them to begin with.

Or perhaps it might be nice to see everyone and hear how their lives played out. Lydia was uncertain about her feelings toward the whole thing.

Still, the level of agitation she was experiencing was without any logical explanation.

Lydia lacked the typical anxieties about status and appearance, yet she still felt self-conscious and unsure. Her green eyes transformed into shades of blue and hazel in the sunlight. She always knew that her green eyes were the rarest in the world, particularly among those of Western European heritage. Aware of her stunning beauty, she had encountered many men who acknowledged it, but Lydia consistently rejected them. Indeed, she didn't feel popular in the past, but it's unclear if anyone truly feels popular in school, regardless of their confidence or social status. Surprisingly, the popular crowd was the most insecure, and the most elite never attended the reunion. Perhaps they chose to maintain their superior image by hiding signs of weight gain and aging.

The educational experience of being torn down by marginally qualified adults and hot-shot peers challenges even the most resilient adolescent self-image. Combine that with playground politics, and you have a condensed form of the worst aspects of international politics. It's not fun for anyone.

The words "high school" evoke an emotional response unrelated to education, years after the anxiety of judgmental peers.

The educational experience is more of a trial to emotionally survive than an academic endeavor, and the system makes less effort to mask that reality with each passing year. Lydia recalled learning that F. Scott Fitzgerald dropped out of college for similar reasons. Lydia endured it but then moved out west and earned a nursing degree in a similar system once more. Despite holding onto the timeless idealistic belief of "We can make a difference," she realized her profession was not her dream job, as it involved encountering its own core political issues and unethical administrators. In addition, her addictions and alcohol consumption led to a rapid transition to prescription drug misuse, which resulted in the swift termination of her job.

The truism about insanity repeating the same plan came to mind when a classmate called her with the invite for the reunion plans. She saw a reunion as a replication of the unsuccessful middle and high school dynamics, where the elite thrived solely due to their wealthy and politically influential parents.

Nevertheless, Lydia might confess to having a twisted curiosity. What happened to those self-centered, egotistical bullies from her youth? You know, the group of kids who always made it known they were from the affluent side of town, which separated towns into two halves: the working middle class and the privileged. Perhaps the emotional turmoil stemmed from encountering friends and rivals, or maybe it was simply the dilemma of accepting the passage of time.

The aging process takes its toll, and even if the new age treatments and creams promise otherwise, we all age and see our elders as we look in the mirror. For many, reunions represent coming to terms with our mortality, emphasized by the aging process. For the bullies and beasts, it's a matter of simply not aging as well as anticipated.

The ability to afford tropical vacations, indulge in fatty foods and sugary drinks, and smoke various products contributes to premature wrinkles in older individuals. It would entail gym visits, dieting, trendy haircuts, and a complete wardrobe makeover. It was tough to be sure. According to her mother, Lydia had gorgeous, chestnut-colored, long hair. At 5'8" and with no weight gain since college, her olive skin remained wrinkle-free. At that moment, it was clear she would probably regret whatever choice she made, just like many of Lydia's other decisions.

Lydia hadn't felt so ridden with anxiety since the last time she set foot in the halls of that school. She regurgitated her entire meal the night she said yes to the reunion. So, why did she agree to the reunion? Reading the newspaper that day while relaxing on the deck, trying to stay sober, her plans changed dramatically when she saw a small picture of Rico, his blond curly hair catching her attention. Rico was attending. These three words drove her forward.

Although Lydia frequently remembered her mother's advice, it was only after her mother's death that she genuinely valued it while disregarding her grandmother's constant reminders to be grateful for their fortunate circumstances in the new homeland.

The Contessa couldn't be stopped as she evangelized about her improved present life compared to her past.

So, Lydia turned to her only adult, her mother, but she, too, had rules and a philosophy that did not stop Lydia's pain. Like most teenagers, Lydia felt her mom was overly protective and too strict, but isn't that a typical feeling during adolescence? Lydia was brought back to her teenage years when her mother taught her about the influence of peer pressure on alcohol and drug use. No alcoholic beverages, including wine and beer, were allowed in their home, even for social events. Her cousins occasionally had wine during family meals, making it extremely tempting to try it.

After Lydia lost her dad, her home life regressed to a small apartment in a four-family house on the west side of the railroad tracks. Sadly, it turned out to be the wrong side, creating a label that implied people from that area were never welcomed into higher education. With determination, she balanced chores and school tasks, all in pursuit of a sports scholarship that would allow her to leave her immigrant community. Whenever she went on dates with local boys, they involved church-sponsored events or going to the local ice cream parlor with a large group of friends, as they were known decades ago.

Lydia and her mother relocated to the West Coast after graduating high school. While her mother worked to support them, Lydia pursued her college education. It didn't take long for them to find out that residents in the old ethnic neighborhoods were not forgiving and would even seek revenge if someone left for a better life. The West was equally lonely, just like the disapproving neighbors back home.

Almost immediately after graduating nursing school, Lydia married Sebastian, a man who would give her a wonderful baby during their second anniversary year. Thomas was adorable and the perfect little toddler, adored by both parents.

Lydia and Sebastian exchanged vows during a simple civil wedding ceremony. Their relationship was uneventful, and their marriage was nothing more than that. Sebastian's interest in his wife was limited to the usual remarks about dinner and his preference for cold beverages. Sebastian was a devoted father and provider who seemed to find joy in parenting, but once Thomas left for college, life became dull for the empty nesters. The marriage was marked by many disappointments, primarily the unfaithfulness of a philandering husband who eventually departed. However, the other perspective is that Lydia, for most of her marriage, battled alcoholism yet managed to function and still be a good mother.

One day, after a double shift nursing job at the hospital, Lydia returned home to a nasty argument about who forgot to pay the electric bill. Lydia could tell this was the moment as she approached Sebastian, who was lounging comfortably on his chair.

"Get up, Sebastian. What color are my eyes?"

"Brown," said Sebastian with some hesitation.

"No, they are green like generations before me," she replied in a monotone of equanimity that equaled her thoughts. "Let's file for divorce." And so they did.

CHAPTER 6

—·—

DECISIONS AND DISQUIETUDE

The decision was carved in stone, and Lydia was on her way to see her friends and former classmates at a ritual known as a reunion. The drive home triggered Lydia's nostalgia as she returned to the suburb where she was born, remembering the exits and roundabouts. Living in the Midwest had its upsides, like beautiful fall foliage and ample snow for winter activities. Lydia, a skilled cross-country skier, relished the solitude and breathtaking views of the trails, yet her mind wandered once more.

Upon entering the suburbs from the south and exiting the interstate, the car filled with the scents of imported cheeses and deli meats from an old European market. Although not made by authentic pizzaiolos, their deep-dish Chicago pizza was still delicious.

Lydia was raised in a suburb near a large, windy city. Returning home in the XKII model rented sports car made everything in the old neighborhood seem smaller. She stopped at a service station with only two pumps to reflect and wash her face with ice-cold water. Lydia's thoughts went to her mother's sage advice in the early years.

Lydia, always remember that you are just as capable as anyone your age, and with hard work and passion, you can achieve anything in life.

Lydia referred to her as Mother and was raised by her as a single parent. But everything took a turn when her father, the beloved son of the Contessa, died young. Lydia's mother was her rock and the most intelligent person she knew. Her mother pleaded for her to focus on the present and leave behind the challenges of high school and college, which were similarly distressing. It was so many years ago, but Lydia's mindset pushed back to her misery as an adolescent.

Regrettably, the pep rally senior year evoked such a vivid image that it caused an audible gasp. Now that she was home, it became an excruciatingly painful ordeal. She had to stop the car and roll down the windows to prevent a complete panic attack.

Lydia buried that thought and the article she

read online deep within her subconscious. Her sole wish was to receive an apology from the individuals who had bullied her in the past. Rico's prominent reputation alerted the media about his upcoming attendance at a hometown reunion. Lydia moved ahead, determined to correct the injustice once more.

What caused Lydia to agree to go to a school reunion with such arrogant and supercilious people? Weren't all schools prone to groups and tribes and gangs? Initially, she had refused the notion of her friends coming together and enjoying themselves, but she sensed it might impact their friendships, and she cherished her friends like family. Contemplating her decision, she wondered why she had said yes to attending the reunion after receiving the phone call. In her hometown's gasoline station, she reflected on her choices and felt regret once more. The flashbacks haunted Lydia, unable to escape their grip once they started.

Her memory took her back to that first phone call months ago. She listened to the answering machine from her balcony, which opened to a view of the moon shining down on the lake off the back deck. It was such a peaceful, warm evening for early March with no wind. The fish were jumping at bugs on the water's surface, and she was at peace with the thought of her planned vacation to go deep-sea fishing the following week. Lydia did not want to disappoint her friends. Saying yes would make her unhappy, while saying no would likely make her friends and former classmates unhappy. What caused her to be so driven by the desire for approval?

She dropped into a chair overlooking the water's edge. A reunion committee chairwoman's voice and encouragement droned on in the background. She returned, speaking a bit louder into her ear this time. "Lydia, can you hear me?" She was determined to make Lydia attend the reunion, reminded her of her previous attendance and refusing to accept no for an answer. It turns out it wasn't about Lydia, but rather, after a few glasses of wine, the classmate confused her with someone from the West Coast.

Sally persisted with the pressure as gossip spread about Lydia's abrupt relocation to California after graduating from high school and, more importantly, what had become of her. The reunion committee's influential classmates told Sally to ensure Lydia attended the reunion. Since there was no response to this line of thinking, Lydia told her she would consider it. Sally hummed a tune from the school games, hoping to bring back happy memories for Lydia, but all Lydia saw was the stadium and the classmates who rejected her.

Her body froze on that lounge chair near the lake. She had come a long way since high school and her hometown. The joys, sorrows, and lessons learned while growing up reminded every cell in her body not to consent to doing something she did not want to do.

Why endure the social pecking order again, which was still alive and kicking?

Enlightenment at such a young age could only result in the gestalt of the true meaning of prejudice. The roots of prejudice and racism were firmly planted in their upbringing, with their homes teaching not only the apparent conflicts between different racial groups but also the exclusion of those who lacked connections or prestigious affiliations from the elite society they had control over.

How can someone who has experienced prejudice hold prejudice against another culture, race, or nationality? When an ethnic joke was told, Lydia didn't even remain in the room. She was completely free from perverse prejudices.

Maybe the experience might be interesting. Among those who compared themselves for years, who ultimately lived a meaningful life, and who pretended? It would address everyone's unanswered questions from graduation years ago.

Lydia finally returned from her thoughts, where all stress-induced disquietude takes place. She decided it was time to retreat to her lake house and end her contemplation of the invitation to the big reunion. Suffering from a throbbing headache, she sought refuge from the storm in her mind by watching an old movie and reliving nostalgic moments.

Lydia contacted her true and real friends to discuss and strategize her next move. Lydia knew which friendships would last a lifetime. Michael, a cousin, Owen, and Joe. They were neighbors and, inspired by an old movie, performed a childhood ritual where they pricked their fingers, drew blood, and became blood brothers and sisters, a commitment they took seriously every day.

Lydia washed her face once more in the gas station, attempting to quiet her constant thoughts as she embarked on a journey to confront her fears and seek justice.

CHAPTER 7

— ◆ —

TRIBE OF FRIENDS

Lydia grew up with a tribe of friends as neighbors, their houses close enough to bike or walk between. It was a great place for everyone to gather and experience the joy of childhood play. Joe lived on the left side of Lydia's backyard, while Owen's house was at a somewhat perpendicular angle. Whenever they had a playdate, Lydia would first go to Joe's house. Afterward, Joe and Lydia would shout for Owen near the small honeysuckle border that separated the properties.

It was probably the honeysuckle that triggered Lydia's allergies. Despite adult warnings, Lydia ignored the risks and tasted the honeysuckle, only to be stung repeatedly by the bees.

So Lydia called Joe first and inquired about his plans to attend the reunion. "Yes, Lydia, we should check out the old place. Of course, we will do this together! Spending time together is worth a weekend away from church work. I look forward to spending quality time with my best friends."

"Sounds great, Joe," Lydia said as she reached for her heart on the other end of the phone. She felt the strange tachycardia only present during an allergic reaction, a pounding that felt as if her heart would indeed break.

Joe had an early calling, knowing he wanted to spend his life serving a higher power. After high school, he was accepted to an elite order, the Jesuits, and they sent him to college.

In his youth, Joe experienced dating, love, and the company of women, but his devotion to his faith was much stronger. Following his calling, he pursued a Jesuit education right after high school and became a Catholic priest.

Joe loved the story of a Spanish nobleman, Ignatius Loyola, from the 16th Century. It seemed that Ignatius had a similar start and enjoyed the company of ladies, flashy clothes, and a life of being revered as a noble, much like Joe! Following a severe war injury, Ignatius was sent to a convent for rehabilitation, where he regained the ability to walk on his injured leg. Ignatius had no choice but to study scripture, and that's when his spiritual awakening started. Recognizing his privileged upbringing and lack of education, Loyola returned to school to learn basic reading and writing skills alongside third-grade boys.

Father Joe told this history so all would value his choices, but Lydia knew he loved Saint Ignatius' sense of spirituality. Loyola climbed the educational ladder and ultimately earned a master's degree with distinction. They let him know he was no longer in his prime at forty-five. Joe greatly admired that lesson the most – the importance of perseverance in education, which led to his remarkable accomplishments and the founding of numerous colleges named after him worldwide. Joe attended one of these institutions of higher learning, then went on to a rigorous education in the monastery before ordination.

Throughout school, the bullies had singled Owen out as a prime target. He was overweight, frequently absent from school, and a victim of relentless bullying that, like Lydia, caused lasting emotional scars. During class changes, he became the target of punches, even though teachers often ignored them.

Joe called him and asked what he thought of the reunion. His response is in two words: "Eleventh grade. Dante had his nine circles of hell. Eleventh grade became my ninth circle. It's that dreadful moment when the last trace of childhood innocence is maliciously torn away and gleefully applauded by spectators who revel in your humiliation." Owen persevered despite almost losing his voice and described eleventh grade as the ninth circle of hell. "It destroyed the final remnants of childhood's idealistic innocence and lingered as a nightmare."

It's hard to believe that forgiving and forgetting is the solution, but there's still a lingering fantasy that we could change the past and ease our suffering. In our darkest, burning dreams, we return and whisper, resist. We need to combat not just bullies but the entire corrupt social structure, where adults witness the daily humiliation and choose to ignore it.

Joe listened with compassion as Owen related a year of traumatic memory. Owen continued, "Let me share a memory. In the first week of school, we were all pushed out of our small, sometimes ethnic, working-class neighborhoods and began our journey in secondary school. I was minding my business at the hallway locker in school, about to leave, when a bully came out of nowhere. The meeting took a violent turn when he delivered a sudden blow to the occipital area from behind that we called a sucker punch. With a laugh, he forcefully slammed my body into a locker, leaving me stunned. As I turned, I saw his twisted, devilish grin and heard his high-pitched laughter while he and his friends continued to assault me with punches and kicks. At that moment, tears were the only response to pain, shock, and humiliation. They forcefully shoved me into a locker and slammed the door."

"They then sauntered on in search of their next victim. The children on both sides of us responded by either shrinking back in fear or cruelly laughing, giving us a glimpse into their world of bullies who torment those from different classes and consider them easy targets for their aggression. The daily humiliations at school, inflicted by a privileged few, introduced me to the ninth circle of hell."

This young teen, who was tormented for years, did not understand the subtexts of it all, of power and class difference, or even of the latent undertone of a perverted hatred. On that day, he remembered walking home alone, in shock and tears, too humiliated to say a word, awakening the next morning with dread. It became a daily repeated of pain, so intense that, at times, he contemplated asking his parents for private school. On his way back to the small row home across town, he stayed alert for the gang of bullies who wanted to give their favorite wimp an additional beating. They would never engage in a fair one-on-one fight, relying on their lamprey-like friends for backup. He didn't realize that he could have defended himself in a one-on-one situation. Fear was their weapon, and fear paralyzed him.

If only he could travel back to that initial week of bullying that established such a terrible pattern for the future. Years of growth and learning have empowered the adult within to guide the twelve-year-old in confronting the abuse.

So that is Owen's fantasy as we head to this damn reunion. The years of torment from bullies and others were our actual reality, but we've moved on and left it behind. The infliction of physical abuse, especially on the males, instilled fear and rendered them immobile.

Imagine a fantasy where we could travel back in time and guide our younger selves for a short period. Therapists often advise us not to dwell on the past, as it cannot be changed. They encourage us to talk about it and eventually move on or even consider the challenging concept of "forgive and forget."

We all contemplate the news about bullying today, especially on the internet. "Tell a teacher, talk to the counselor, ask for help." Perhaps it would have helped Lydia and Owen, but the cold sweats in the middle of the night did not stop.

CHAPTER 8

CHANGE MY MIND

Lydia could not resist the urge to call Owen and Father Joe repeatedly about the reunion. It completely consumed her. They talked and tried to convince her that things would work out. They would stand beside her and help make the weekend pass smoothly. Unbeknownst to her, the events that would unfold that weekend would be shattering and dangerous for all three of them.

Should Lydia choose to go, she would meet her demise, prompting us, her friends, to uncover the reasons behind it. As we delved into the depths of high school's gladiatorial pit, our initial half-serious quest to unravel its secrets took a dangerous turn when we realized that suicide didn't quite add up.

Joe and Owen agreed about Lydia's amazing future

and her role as a wonderful friend. Boys from all socio-economic groups noticed her as a teenager because she was strikingly beautiful. She loved high school sports and was present at every away game. Our love for football, basketball, and baseball strengthened our friendships.

We enjoyed the traditional bonfire pep rally. The friends would gather on the field around the huge bonfire and enjoy the songs and shouts of a hopeful victory the next day against the rival teams from neighboring cities.

Joe and Owen vividly remember one cold evening in November in senior year as we sat as close to the fire as possible to mitigate the chill in the air, noticing Lydia was without a coat. She appeared to be drinking with some of the guys from the team and was plenty warm from whatever was in that flask. Usually, the crew surrounding her didn't socialize with her or her friends. They were, after all, lettered men, worn on their sweaters to inform us. They rarely spoke to anyone other than others like themselves who were headed to top colleges in the fall. The adults also enjoyed their company more than supervisors should. They were the leaders of the winning team, and their athletes were the elite who secured the wins, giving them high status.

We saw Lydia walk off toward the stadium with Rico within the hour. His steady girlfriend was not there that night. We had cold chills running up our arms, making our hair stand on edge as we watched. The stadium area was known as Lover's Lane, and only heavy-kissing couples ventured there during the pep rally. Cheating with the co-captain while his girlfriend was not around was not wise.

On that cool November day, Rico asked Lydia to join him, "Here, try my drink to warm you up, Lydia. It is delicious, and I'd love to hang out with you."

As Lydia drank from his flask, the bonfire flames shot thirty feet in the air, smelling of pine wood and crackling like a Christmas Eve fireplace. After a few cups of the warm liquid Rico had provided, Lydia looked up to see Joe and Owen walking by, but they did not speak, as the group she had joined was not welcoming.

Lydia needed some help as her drinking was catching up with her. Rico was happy to hold her up, "Take my arm, Lydia, and I'll help you to the stadium bathrooms." Her head spinning a little in her seat, Rico attentively took her arm and helped her cut through the crowds to the bathrooms behind the bleachers.

Lydia began her words, "Rico, you are so handsome

and smell so good. I have always loved your curly blonde hair. My mother was so wrong about you." Lydia was no longer ambulatory at this point but made one last attempt to express her needs. "Rico, please get me to the bathroom door."

It was never part of Rico's plan to help Lydia anywhere. Gripping her arm, he pulled her toward a wooded area and said, "It's easier to just pee in the woods." With a sudden flash of sobriety, Lydia resisted.

Then, the sudden force of feeling Rico slap her face with the full force of an adult male sent her spinning to the ground. Lydia's last recollection was of male laughter and jokes similar to those from "Right of the First Knight." Lydia gazed up at Rico, meeting his deep brown eyes, and softly asked, "Rico, why?" She saw an adult wildly waving his hands and arms until they disappeared into the escape plan of their sycophant.

Lydia ran the shower until it went cold, and the next morning, she told her mother everything. "Mom, it was so stupid to trust them." Lydia and her mother went to the police and the school principal, but no one believed her. Once she confessed to being drunk, everyone assumed she made up the story, so Rico was never questioned or investigated. Rico had again avoided consequences for his vulgar actions. Mother suggested they pack it up and begin the journey to their new life in California.

Rico was a popular fellow and an influencer if we had used that term back then. He was the sly, silent type. Captain of the teams and in like Flynn with the educators who practically wrote his college admission ticket. He would attend a prestigious college and later secure a high–ranking role in his father's company. His father owned a major used car company, where a handful of dishonest salesmen made millions for the business and its subsequent franchises. Regardless of the salesmen's high yearly earnings (which is never sufficient for them), they were willing to take illicit kickbacks to sell specific cars to their customers.

Before regulations, Rico's dad established a corner lot business selling used cars. The vehicle costs were exaggerated, odometers were tampered with, and unfair loan installment programs were established, burdening clients even after the vehicle was sold for parts. Rico increased his income by importing and exporting stolen luxury vehicles, which resulted in significantly higher profits for those willing to buy and modify the cars.

Rico had it easy by the time he inherited the business. All he had to do was modernize the less ethical practices and look forward to making more money than he could ever spend. He did this by sitting in a plush office suite, viewing potential auto purchases around the globe, and importing those with the best markup. Polished at sales and marketing, he sat with each potential client, convincing them that image was everything. The perfect exotic automobile sent a message of success. Yes, deception was alive and well, and, of course, Rico would benefit from it.

With little effort, the family achieved astonishing profits and joined the ranks of the nouveau riche. Morally bankrupt criminal activity by manipulators ruined the integrity of an ethical industry. Welcome to the real world.

No one was indicted for misconduct. The board of directors made a considerable amount of money. This firm belonged to Rico, and eventually, he took charge of it. How do we know this story? An axiom claims there are two routes to generational wealth—to inherit or steal it. Some individuals manage to do both, thanks to nepotism and malicious intent.

One could argue that things never change after high school. Even in retirement, the pecking order remains intact, with few realizing the community is more than just background characters in their life. This statement especially applies to those who view themselves as superior by their birthright in the USA. While a mugger would threaten you with a gun, Rico used a smile and a handshake to deceive you under the guise of a favor. In a culture built on illusion and manipulation, it's not surprising that Rico embraced his solipsistic nature.

Rico's daily routine consisted of waking up, reading the news, analyzing business data, selling high-end vehicles, enjoying lavish meals, playing golf, and indulging in occasional massages. He received an incredibly high annual salary for rendering those services.

It was a back-slapping career for Rico. He taught his salesmen the finer techniques with the lines of: "Hello, Mr. Gullible! How's everything going? Oh, what's that? You say you went to the dentist today? Whoa! The dentist! How about that? Oh, you just stumbled onto some insurance money that was paid out when your brother accidentally fell from his lawnmower? Let me show you a luxury vehicle you can't afford and won't help you accomplish your goals, but it pays me an incredible amount." And on they go to the appropriate sales script. There's a gullible person born every minute.

Rico's personality would never entertain the idea of working long hours for an average income. Hard work would be a complete waste of time. The reason is that if a man puts in effort, he might eventually be able to afford that ocean-view condo, even if it's in the distant future. In retirement, the partner may receive the condo and possibly the house and cars as part of the divorce settlement – it's unpredictable. Living out retirement feeling broken, barely getting by in an adult community, or worse, working a job for minimal pay until age eighty-two. This is how Rico viewed the middle class. The average person's journey to retirement is lengthy, but by taking advantage of others and stepping on as many people as necessary, that journey can be shorter.

There is, however, an unusual reality that persists through the class divide in America: the very rich and the very poor behave in ways that are, for the most part, eerily similar. Yacht parties and diner parties typically follow a comparable pattern: overindulging in red meat and alcohol and the opportunity to exchange contact details for possible infidelity.

The wealthy can use nicer cars when attending their divorce hearings, which might be their goal. In the meantime, the chase persists for everyone involved. The wealthy continue to believe they are superior to those without the same advantages, oblivious to the irony. Should the general population somehow realize the pointlessness of material greed, the societal factions will still clash.

The extent to which people are willing to fight over sports teams, even over something as trivial as the color of their jerseys, suggests they would go to even greater extremes in higher-stakes situations. If a ball over a fence is one point, what is the point value for Rico and similar individuals who make the rich richer, disappointing those who once believed in the American dream?

It's human nature to delude ourselves into a good-versus-evil worldview, where we always play the role of a good guy. It's possibly a more accurate description of humanity than the altruistic version embraced by do-gooders and those who feign to be do-gooders. Many of those individuals judge others' morals while simultaneously degrading the moral values of their families, communities, and workplaces. However, the modern elites would never concern themselves with moral or character dilemmas, which creates a contradiction for the less privileged.

CHAPTER 9

— · —

THE SOULMATES

"Daddy, can you buy me a fruit cup? And an apple, too?"

Thomas stood at the railing of the zoo's silverback gorilla exhibit with his 8-year-old daughter, Sophia.

"How about a hot dog instead?"

"No. Just a fruit cup," she replied. "Hot dogs are gross."

"You know, these fellas are herbivores. That means they only eat plants, but look how big they get. The male over there is four hundred, maybe four hundred and fifty pounds," Thomas said, gesturing at the enclosure. "Silverback gorillas don't have many predators in the wild, but humans hunt them for sport and trophies. That's the biggest threat to their survival. Did they teach you about Dian Fossey in school?"

Sophia shook her head no.

"Dian Fossey dedicated her life to studying gorillas. While protecting them from poachers, she ended up being murdered. But she died for something she believed in, protecting animals she loved when they couldn't protect themselves. That's what makes life meaningful," Thomas posited. By then, Sophia's attention had already been drawn to a neighboring exhibit. She pulled her father by the hand to the monkeys, beckoning for attention.

A doting father, Thomas achieved the "I'm going to give her all that I never had growing up" goal of most parents raised in less-than-stellar financial and nurturing circumstances. Sophia attended a private school, had many friends, and displayed early signs of inheriting her father's analytical mind, her mother's artistic talent, and her moral idealism. Her knowledge of her father's childhood struggles was limited, and Thomas had no intention of revealing them to her anytime soon.

As a young man, Thomas' parents attempted to downplay his ethnic heritage. They reminded him, You're an American. Remember the sacrifices to come to America and value the opportunity to be here.

Thomas was fluent in three languages, including the basic Italian he learned from his mother, Lydia. However, both parents discouraged him from speaking anything but English in the household. Southern California was far from the melting pot of ethnic and interracial culture as it is now, and Thomas had felt his share of discrimination growing up. Kids shunned him for being of a different ethnic background, and he was mocked for acting too ethnic.

With his parents prizing education above all else, Thomas had little interest in being another of the West's ubiquitous Scarface clones. It was a no-win situation, and he dreamed of leaving for the tolerance and deep cultural diversity of a new city, states away.

His wish came true when he was admitted to his dad's alma mater in the East for college. With books and writing as his refuge and haven during childhood, he wasted no time choosing to pursue a pre-law major. In his daydreams, he imagined using the law as a platform to rectify all the injustices he had endured, composing legal briefs with heartfelt words, and resolving the world's issues through his typewriter.

Thomas' work in college bore the watermark of his idealism, regardless of how much effort his professors made to soften his tone. College newspapers are, after all, a joint venture between truth-telling and truth-manipulating, and Thomas was one of the few of his peers who would have nothing to do with the latter. Although this garnered him respect for his integrity, it also caused him difficulties from those who perceived him as a renegade. He wasn't the ideal company man. He took it personally whenever he thought the company's bottom line was prioritized over the betterment of the community it purported to serve. Unsurprisingly, his interest in exposing this injustice meant he had plenty of targets for his often scathing writing.

"C'mon, let's go to the cafe," Thomas said, taking Sophia's hand. "I'll buy you a hot dog. Oops, I mean a fruit cup."

"Ok, Daddy, but call Mommy to meet us. I like holding her hand and yours on the other."

"Good plan, honey!"

As Cathleen and Thomas walked onto the beach, he took her hands and looked lovingly into her eyes.

"Cathleen, I've received a job offer as an assistant to the district attorney in the county where my mother grew up, back in the Midwest. My investigations received more attention than expected, and they appreciated my style. Making the move means our lives will be altered, and we will leave behind the sunny West Coast as a distant memory."

"Honey, college will always hold a special place in our hearts where we fell in love. Thomas, let's make this change for our daughter's sake, as it will introduce her to new experiences and help her learn." Cathleen held Thomas' hand and placed it on her abdomen. "We will do this together." Her smile was radiant, an obvious reflection of her love. "Thomas, we are a family and a growing one."

Thomas gazed into Cathleen's eyes. "This is fantastic news!" Aware that their love had brought forth a new life, he smiled, capturing the profound amazement of how things could turn out very well.

CHAPTER 10

—·—

BY THE SEA

The vicissitudes of Grandma Lydia's death might have been the catalyst for Thomas and Cathleen to leave California and start new lives in the Midwest. Still, the wonders of the move were extraordinary. Thomas' private legal practice eventually became very lucrative, allowing him to buy a beachfront vacation house on the eastern coast.

Cathleen developed into an amazing watercolor artist. She was near the jetty almost daily, painting the marvelous crashing sea waves. Talented, gifted, and a wonderful mother, she remembered that her love for Thomas had crafted an idyllic life, and she adored him. They were indeed soulmates.

Their family beach house became a haven and

a wonderful mindful time for family adventures. Sophia flourished in California, loving her attachment to the boogie board. The stress of their lives melted away as they immersed themselves in the calming ocean waves. Thomas, Cathleen, their daughter Sophia, and her love, Philip, prepared for a joyful beach outing with additional family members.

The meals were organized while the board games rested beside the surfboards and fishing poles. The return of their lovely daughter from college was a cause for celebration. Cousin Michael and his wife Joan were also guests. Michael, a military retiree, arrived early to join the family celebrations. They all witnessed Sophia and their young son, Ricky, walking near the jetty in sight of their beachfront home.

Bringing up the rear, Sophia's boyfriend, Philip, enjoyed the sensation of sinking his toes into the warm sand as they walked on the beach.

"Sophia, we need to catch up with your little brother. He is way out there on the jetty."

With a slight chuckle, she said, "You are overprotective, Philip, but I am in awe of your love for my family."

"Walking on the beach with you and your little

brother this morning, holding hands, has inspired me to ask your parents for permission to marry you. I deeply love you, and you've already said yes. Sophia, should we approach them today at the barbecue?"

Although Sophia smiled, her hesitation showed Phil that it might not be the right moment, knowing she would be lectured about completing college at age twenty. "Your cousin, Michael, may grasp the situation, but parents are usually reluctant to see their children take the independent leap into marriage and start their own lives."

Sophia suggested they enjoy the present moment while watching the waves crash against the jetty.

The East has noticeably warmer water, not to mention tranquil beaches with gorgeous white sand. Simply walking along the beach can unexpectedly teach one profound knowledge about the world and its humble inhabitants.

Philip, Sophia, and Ricky were having such a walk along a sparsely populated shore when they stumbled upon many male and female horseshoe crabs mating in the warm May weather. The moist sand served as a nesting ground for the female's eggs. The pre-historic rituals of this primitive arthropod, affectionately called a living fossil, date back almost a billion years, adding to its paradox.

To show Ricky the crab's structure, Philip carefully lifted one, being cautious not to touch the tail, which plays a crucial role in the crab's ability to overturn. "Remember, Rick, if the horseshoe crab's tail is damaged, the little fellow could not maneuver and flip. The horseshoe crab is not a crab at all. It's an arthropod and invertebrate with no spine."

Ricky's smile resembled a young preteen who had just received car keys. He was thrilled to be called Rick and determined to follow in his footsteps.

Sophia entered the conversation and used the teachable moment with Ricky.

"Ricky, the eggs that survive undergo several molting stages until fully mature." Sophia kept going as Ricky sat beside a big crab on the sand. "The horseshoe crab produces a life-saving substance used in biotechnology that impacts nearly everyone who has visited a doctor or hospital."

Like clockwork, Michael came jogging by and joined the conversation, always in teaching mode. Ricky had immense respect for his parents and elders. But he held his dad's cousin Michael in such high regard because of the countless life lessons he had learned from him.

Philip carried on, feeling the need to delve deeper

into the subject. "The liquid comes from horseshoe crabs worldwide and is harvested in laboratories. The horseshoe crabs are removed from the beaches and transported to labs, where they are laid on their sides. A device is connected close to their hearts to draw out their blood. Just one quart of this liquid is valued at thousands of dollars. The crabs are immediately returned to the sea to ensure their gills remain wet."

Michael noticed Ricky's face taking on a sad expression and sought help from Sophia to rescue him from that gloomy statement. Sophia contributed by sharing her perspective on the discussion.

"Ricky, picture it this way," examining both sides or embracing a Zen middle path. "The researchers are constantly working to create a synthetic alternative for bleeding the crabs. The value of the liquid blue blood is essential to medical science. Anyone receiving a routine injection at the doctor's office or injectables for insulin, knee replacements, or the use of hospital instruments is safer from life-threatening infections thanks to our little horseshoe crab friends."

"Oh, I get it. The liquid is a sterilization thing better than heat."

"Exactly, Rick."

As a marine biologist, Philip felt compelled to conclude this fantastic topic. "The horseshoe crab swims on its back most of the year to migrate to sand or mud. In spring, the female eggs are fertilized by several males, and years later, they grow, molt, and emerge in the same area of their birth. Unlike many other pre-historic creatures, they have survived for millions of years because of their protective bloodstream, preventing the ocean bacteria from causing their extinction. Unlike vertebrates, horseshoe crabs lack hemoglobin. They use hemocyanin to transport oxygen, resulting in their blood appearing blue because of the presence of copper."

"Okay, Philip. I think we are way ahead of Ricky's question, but I am sure he would love to learn what we can do to help them survive." Sophia had the instincts of a motherly older sister.

"So, Ricky, we can turn them over after finding them on the sand in the sun so they can make their way back to the water. It's called flipping the horseshoe crab." Philip gently lifted the beautiful arthropod as Ricky watched and joined him to flip dozens on the beach that day. They returned to the beach house and sat down to a magnificent family meal fit for a Contessa.

The move to the east after Grandma Lydia's

untimely death opened a new world for Sophia. She thrived and excelled in academics and athletics. Many of the horrors that Grandma faced were no longer in existence. The bullies of previous times were punished upon appearing, or maybe the newer generation of teenagers was just more empathetic.

At Lydia's funeral, Sophia realized the truth of Zen's teachings about staying in the present, which she had learned years ago. Mindfulness and meditation were integral to her life, and meeting Philip in a campus Zen group was a bonus. They shared a physical and spiritual bond and spent time together, embracing open-mindedness without judgment. With his attractive appearance, athletic physique, and brilliant mind, Philip was the ideal candidate for young love.

Despite her success as a champion field hockey player, Sophia's passion for academics led her to pursue an English major. In her pursuit of becoming a writer, Sophia concealed her ideas for the great American novel, as all great authors do.

Philip was a senior and was on his way to graduate school next year for the master's/doctoral program in marine biology. Hand in hand, they planned a life together on the beach, optimistic yet maintaining their individuality.

Thomas and Cathleen instilled values, ethics, and commitment, forming the tight-knit family now heading to the beach house. They had an enormous meal waiting for them. It was a Sunday tradition where they connected and communicated, unlike anything in today's society.

Thomas, Michael, and their wives joined the elders on an early trip to the market for ripe tomatoes, cheeses, and antipasto meats. By utilizing all senses, the tomato is first visually perceived, then physically felt, and ultimately subjected to the sniff test. The plum tomatoes must be the correct size and color to achieve the perfect lasagna. "Thomas, grab some more for the salad as I chat with the butcher." Each new generation verbally passes down the wisdom of this ancient tradition, using a pinch instead of a teaspoon. The Contessa's presence was palpable.

The main course, enjoyed by Italians and Italian food lovers, was the traditional and delicious lasagna. It featured wide, flat noodles layered with ricotta cheese, parsley, and chopped turkey meat.

The obligatory salumi was still served, the prosciutto, sopressata, genoa salami, and capicola. Because of cholesterol concerns, these were served in smaller amounts than the ancestors ate them. The Fiorentina T-bone steak was placed on the barbecue for five minutes on each side. Served medium rare, it stimulated anticipation and salivation. This steak came from the Chianina cows in Tuscany and had to be imported. The generous portions of broccoli rabe completed the meal.

Thomas rose to propose a toast to the Contessa Angelina. She was the modern-day matriarch who taught us to practice gratitude. Salute!

"Michael, would you like to join us in reminiscing about a beautiful memory from when my mother was a teenager at one of the Contessa's dinners?"

"I'll start, Mike. I think I have it memorized. When my mother, Lydia, was a young teen, Contessa Angelina asked her to write about how our family celebrated the Feast of the Seven Fishes. She also expected Michael to contribute, so he invited his dad to translate any Italian."

"Exactly, Thomas," Michael smiled, producing the index cards loaded with food stains from his backpack. "This is the authentic record of why and how we celebrated as an unofficial feast started in Naples and brought to America."

Sophia interjected, revealing her college research that the tradition of the Seven Fishes Meals on Christmas Eve wasn't mentioned in American literature until the 1980s. "Wrong, honey. Look at the dates on your Grandma Lydia's recipe cards; Michael was there! It was the Christmas of 1964." The room went silent as we all stood to view the dates and cards. "Wow, so that's the truth. Leave it to the Contessa to trust Grandma Lydia to give us this gem," Sophia smiled with pride. "In fact, this dates back to the 19th century in Italy. The Contessa left this as one of her legacies."

"So, who wants to head to the boardwalk to exercise after this wonderful meal and have a soft-serve ice cream while we walk?"

Ricky was the first to respond. "Sounds fun. Is there any chance for cotton candy, too, Dad?"

"Yes, tonight is celebratory, but first, your mother has a surprise." Cousin Michael walked in with his hands full of things and passed them to Cathleen and Thomas. Cathleen was holding tickets and announced the next family reunion would be in Paris at the Olympics!

Thomas asked the family if they should extend the trip to visit the renovated ruins of the new Pompeii and accept Michael and Joan's invitation to stay at their vacation home near Naples.

The family reflected on their gratitude and equanimity, recognizing their generational progress and individual growth. By following ancient traditions, they could escape the hedonic treadmill and find happiness in their love for others. Sophia suggested grabbing their jackets as the boardwalk had a chilly breeze from the ocean at night, and off they all went.

CHAPTER 11

— · —

TRANQUILITY 2019~2022

Confident the perfect life is happening around the globe!

AFTERWORD

The young do not know enough to be prudent, and therefore they attempt the impossible –

and achieve it, generation after generation.

~ Pearl S. Buck

ACKNOWLEDGEMENTS

I met my husband, Dr. David, for the first time on Christmas Eve. He had traveled from medical school in the Midwest with a cousin to explore the East Coast. Despite being raised in California, he was eager to visit Washington, DC, New York City, and Philadelphia. However, when he entered my home, we were immediately drawn to each other. We visited Washington, DC, and Philadelphia together the following day. Our engagement occurred a few years later, on Christmas Eve. We married the following year. I am delighted to dedicate this book to my husband, the most incredible person I have ever met.

As a young intern and resident, he displayed exceptional brilliance and compassion, which continued throughout his entire career without exception. He taught medical students, conducted research, and worked for a medical school and one of the largest laboratories in America. Renowned as a doctor's doctor, he was a pathologist who consistently provided precise information to clinicians to enhance their healing endeavors. While undertaking a Fellowship at USC Medical School in California, he developed a monoclonal antibody revolutionizing the diagnosis of Hodgkin's disease.

Despite his crucial contributions, he remained humble, often working behind the scenes, never meeting the patients directly. His dedication was evident through his long hours and being available for calls from other physicians at any hour of the day. His extraordinary skills and healing nature have persisted even in retirement.

ABOUT THE AUTHOR

Nora D'Ecclesis, a distinguished author, graduated from Kean University and now lives in Pennsylvania. Her award–winning publications cover a wide range of topics, including spirituality, mindfulness, Zen meditation, gratitude, and equanimity.

TESTIMONIALS

"Blending historical narrative with dramatic flair, The Contessa's Legacy by Nora D'Ecclesis is a tale of lives interwoven into a tapestry, distanced by centuries and bridged by the spirit of resilience and traditional legacy. From the ancient ruins of Pompeii to refuge in Naples, the narrative leapfrogs centuries ahead to the streets of America, introducing the life of Contessa Angelina, an old noblewoman thrust by circumstances as an immigrant in America. Balancing her Italian culture with the bursting democratic American soil, she becomes a bridge for the family to their culture and traditions. As if echoing through generations, struggles faced by Contessa in modern America resonate through her oldest granddaughter, Lydia, whose personal and societal struggles with bullying and social acceptance create an inner battle that mirrors the volcanic disruptions faced by her ancestors centuries ago. An emotional core to the narrative, Lydia's poignant story revolves around resolving her battles of the past, trying to find catharsis and closure of the devastation in her inner landscape. Could ancient Pompeii, undone by volcanic fury and unfinished tales, seek resolution through its descendants? The story explores how people view their lasting legacies in various ways: some consider them a burden, while others find them inspiring. The juxtaposition of tradition and change in the narrative mirrors the societal dynamics. In portraying Contessa's embrace of her traditions on American soil and Lydia's internal struggle against imposed values, the text reflects the clash between cultural assimilation and traditional preservation. The narrative here points to a balance between a way of life that honors the past while shaping the future."

Quill says: "The Contessa's Legacy is a compelling and affecting story targeted at readers interested in intricate narratives spanning different eras and contemporary issues. Illuminating the enduring power of the human spirit of resilience, it radiates the themes of identity and the impact of history on the present life."

~ Tripti Kandari, The Feathered Quill

"The Contessa's Legacy describes the lives of generations of a family that immigrated to America. Like all generations, they experience love, disappointment, class prejudice, clashes of cultures, and the joy that comes from continuing many of the traditions of their ethnic culture. The story includes descriptions of lavish family meals where you can almost smell and taste the wonderful feast at the table. As someone with an interest in zen, I enjoyed Nora's beautifully written funeral chapter as well as giving a succinct overview of zen practice and how it can peacefully inform and enrich our spiritual lives."

~ Thane Lawrie, Author and CEO

***

"Although it is a novella, I felt like I knew this family and the characters well, which is a testament to the skillful writing by D'Ecclesis. She shared enough to draw me in and keep me engaged, enjoying every piece of information about the history and experiences of the characters. I enjoyed the focus on Italy and learning about the significance of food in celebrations and family get-togethers. The

Contessa's Legacy is well-structured, easy to read, delightful, fascinating, and timeless. It is the kind of book you can pick in any decade, and the plot will remain entertaining, and the core message will remain relevant."

~ Jennie Moore- Readers' Favorites, 5 Star

***

"I'm amazed at how D'Ecclesis managed to tell the stories of people from multiple generations of an Italian-American family within such a limited word count. The author uses a minimalistic prose style and packs a lot into a fast-paced narrative to deliver an epic and engaging tale that celebrates the resilient nature of the human spirit. The characters are compelling, but this is primarily a theme-driven story and is all the more enjoyable for that. While Lydia's fate might break your heart, Angelina's story will inspire a broad range of readers. Highly recommended."

~ Pikasho Deka, Journalist The Concord Monitor, NH

"The story is well-crafted and has elements of realism that evoke nostalgia and make you reflect on significant historical moments. I loved that Nora D'Ecclesis paid meticulous attention to details and created well-developed characters. Readers will relate to each character and their struggles and find solace in the fact that they are not alone. The book also explores aspirations and dreams, inspiring readers to envision their future and motivating them to reach their goals. I enjoyed this book because it entertained me and inspired introspection."

~ Doreen Chombu, Writer: International Business Times and Readers' Favorite

***

"The Contessa's Legacy: A Novella is a delightful and thought-provoking read. Historically accurate we are treated to glimpses of past cultures and traditions. Nora has captured the essence of a great family and the importance of what is passed down to their future generations.

This is a book that spans centuries. A book that speaks of major changes in fortunes, in movements to different areas and countries and societies. Yet , it is a book about consistency, about acceptance of what is, and a story of bringing the most important family traditions to the next generation despite the fickle movement of the Wheel of Fortune.

D'Ecclesis Contessa's Legacy is the place where the past meets the present, where the present traditions are carried to the future with love and confidence by the next generation. From family holiday food traditions to the weekly family meetings over Sunday dinner. The safety and sense of family permeates, the warmth and comfort of knowing the path was not always easy, but the family has the solid foundation to overcome any difficulties, because their traditions have ensured their survival and the Contessa's offspring many, many years later can face the future with the confidence, love, and hope that has sustained their family through all those generations."

~ Dr. Maria T. Bohle. USA and Tuscany, Italy

***

"Normally, I'm not a fan of ancient historical reads, but something drew me into this story that begins in 79 AD with the eruption of Mt. Vesuvius. Perhaps it took me back to school as I tried to remember what I knew about the subject. It turned out it wasn't much, so I was led on an exploring expedition through Google. Perhaps it was the fact that I have been a genealogist for forty years and family connections through the years fascinate me.

This author weaves a narrative beginning with Marcus and Julia's planned wedding in Pompeii to the family's escape from the eruption to Naples by ship. Generations later members of this family tree led them to America and an Italian America settlement.

I love looking back on family trees to see how and why we end up where we did, and this story took this family farther than I could ever have imagined. This is an intriguing view of how history and its evolving events affects us all.

I also enjoyed the narrative style of Patricia Rullo. She made listening to the audio very easy and pleasant."

~ Michigander - Amazon 5 Star Review

***

"The beautifully written Contessa's Legacy, written by Nora D'Ecclesis describes the joy of Contessa Angelina's first taste of her beloved

Margherita Pizza in America. It was named after Queen Margherita of Savoy, the Queen of Italy. The Queen requested Chef Raffaele Esposito prepare a pizza for her historical royal visit to Naples. He prepared three, but her favorite was the one with the thin, red San Marzano plum tomatoes, mozzarella, and fresh basil, which beautifully represented the Italian flag and its unification. As a result, the Chef named it after the Queen. The ingredients used in the dish are sourced exclusively from Campania, the area surrounding Naples, and this tradition continues. The pizzaiolo prepares by gathering the ingredients as all good chefs do in the initial phases of preparation.

The province of Caserta in the Campania region, near Naples, is where Italian water buffalo are found. They provide the milk that is used to create the exquisite milky mozzarella cheese. Hand-cutting is the traditional way of separating mozzarella cheese from the curds in Italy, resulting in a distinctively flavorful and silky texture, complemented by a hint of salt. The plum tomatoes, known as San Marzano, have a thin and pointed shape and are cultivated beneath Mt. Vesuvius. Similarly, the fresh basil used in the restaurants is a green heirloom variety that is grown outside the restaurants in direct sunlight.

The ingredients include:

Bread flour (4.25 cups)

Water (2.5 cups)

Yeast (.03 oz.)

Sea salt (2 Tbsp)

Sugar (pinch)

Peeled San Marzano plum tomatoes (14 oz.)

Water buffalo mozzarella (3.53 oz.)

Extra virgin olive oil

Fresh green basil

Mix the yeast, salt, and sugar in the usual way until dissolved. Then, very slowly, add the flour to form a pizza dough. Transfer to the board and knead the dough back and forth with your hands, never using a rolling pin. Cover with a wet cloth overnight, then make it into a few balls.

Stretch the dough on the pizza pan using your fingertips to fit the pan, just like it's been done for generations. Then, flip the dough and stretch again, following the time-honored technique.

The peeled San Marzano tomatoes are crushed by hand and spread around the center of the pizza, leaving about an inch around the edges or circumference of the dough without tomatoes. Then, place torn pieces of green basil and buffalo mozzarella in a daisy–circle fashion directly on the tomatoes, followed by a drizzle of extra virgin olive oil.

The type of oven will determine the baking time, but typically, it will be about two minutes in a wood fire until black veins can be seen under the crust. In a traditional oven, bake at 475 degrees for about five minutes.

Add whole green basil leaves to the pizza before serving to enhance the flavor. Garlic and oregano are not part of the ingredients. Divide the pizza into four equal slices and place a large piece on the plate. Because the crust is so pliable, simply fold it over twice and enjoy your slice by hand; no utensils are necessary.

This is the authentic Margherita Pizza that Contessa enjoys in the novel and teaches to the next generation.

I highly recommend this novel."

~ "Let's Eat!" - David Pham, Food Vlogger known as "Mcgiddyphafat" an Influencer on Instagram and YouTube.

Made in the USA
Middletown, DE
06 March 2025

72345718R00075